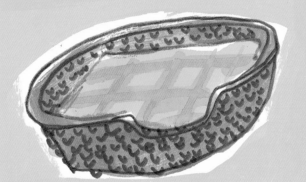

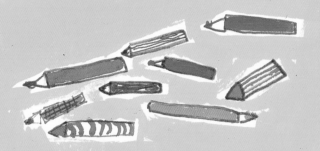

FOR DAD AND MY FIRST BOX OF CRAYONS. NL

FOR LAURA, WHO POINTED OUT THAT OUR CAT SMUDGE THOUGHT WE WERE HER PET HUMANS - MR

A DOUBLEDAY BOOK FOR YOUNG READERS

Published by
RANDOM HOUSE, INC.
1540 Broadway, New York, New York 10036
Doubleday and the portrayal of an anchor with a dolphin are trademarks of
Random House, Inc.

Text copyright © 1999 by Michael Rosen
Illustrations copyright © 1999 by Neal Layton
First American Edition 1999
First published in Great Britain by Bloomsbury, 1999

Cataloging-in-Publication Data is available from the U.S. Library of Congress.
ISBN: 0-385-32677-7

The text of this book is set in 26.5-point Providence Sans.
Manufactured in Belgium
June 1999
10 9 8 7 6 5 4 3 2 1

ROVER

Written by

Michael Rosen  Neal Layton

illustrated by

A DOUBLEDAY BOOK FOR YOUNG READERS

T

his is my pet human. Humans come in all sizes. She's the kind who's a bit bigger than me. I named her Rover.

Her ears are not as good as mine.
She has very weak claws.
Her coat only covers her head.

Her dad, whom I call Rex, has coat on his face.
Her mom, whom I call Cindy, doesn't.

Sometimes I sit on Rover. Sometimes Rover sits on Cindy. Sometimes Rover sits on Rex. Sometimes we all sit on each other.

Rover doesn't eat her food properly. She pokes it with metal things.

At night I take her to her basket. It's very long and when she's in it she hides under a cushion with small bears.

I let her have a rabbit as well, though I would like it in my basket.

Rover's bark is very squeaky. Sometimes my friends bring over some other small humans. Since they're all so young, we think it's all right if they bark a lot together.

When Rover and I go to the park, she keeps losing her ball, but I always bring it back for her.

She spends a lot of time watching a loud, colored box. When she's bored with it, I wag my tail and she watches that instead.

In the summer I lead them to the family box and Rex and Cindy move it very quickly to the seashore. I help it go faster by putting my head out the window.

VROOm!

We go to an enormous sandpit, where the humans rip off lots of their clothes. Then some of them run around like crazy, and some lie down and pretend to be dead.

One day last summer we sat in the sandpit while the wind blew the sand all over us. I liked it but Rex and Cindy didn't. In the end they fell asleep on a blanket.

Near our spot, a man and a woman were trying to eat each other. That was when Rover went for a walk toward the rocks. I was sad to see her getting smaller and smaller until she disappeared.

Then Rex got up from his blanket.
He stood and looked up and down
the sandpit.
    He woke Cindy and they
both started barking.

Cindy rushed over to the people eating each other and started pointing all over the sandpit and barking some more. Then they all looked at me.

Rex waved Rover's rabbit under my nose
and barked. It was getting very loud and all the
people who had been lying down stood up. Cindy
gave me a pat.

I thought it was time to go back to the box, but I didn't want to go without Rover. So I walked off down the sandpit to fetch her.

Rex and Cindy walked behind me. They kept looking at the sea.
   Every human we walked past, they barked at.

One group was trying to smash a ball into a net. Sometimes they missed and it went over. Then they barked a lot.
I couldn't see Rover.

Rex and Cindy were breathing loudly and they had more lines than usual on their faces.

We got to the rocks. In between the rocks were large puddles. In the puddles were stupid things with eight legs that walked sideways.

Rex and Cindy wanted to go back and tried to make me go with them. I thought that was a bad idea because we had come to get Rover.

I jumped over the rocks.
I couldn't see Rover.
I looked back. Lots of people were standing at the end of the sandpit waving their arms. Rex and Cindy were squeezing each other.

Then I jumped over one more rock and there was Rover staring into a puddle.

I barked. She looked at me and pointed at one of those stupid eight-legged things. I barked again, and Rex and Cindy came over the top of the rock and started barking and howling. Their eyes were all watery and they rushed up to Rover and picked her up.

Soon we headed back. Cindy and Rex kept patting me all over and rubbing my neck. Rex kept showing Rover's rabbit to everyone and pointing at me.

At last we could all get in the box and go home.

And I thought: Next time Rover starts getting smaller and smaller, I'll chase after her to keep her nice and big.